The
Nicest
Naughtiest
Fairy

Nick Ward

HUTTON hg GROVE

written and illustrated by
Nick Ward

The Nicest Naughtiest Fairy

The Nicest Naughtiest Fairy
Text Copyright · Nick Ward
Illustration Copyright · Nick Ward
The rights of Nick Ward to be named as the author and illustrator of this
work have been asserted by them in accordance with the Copyright,
Designs and Patents Act, 1988

Published in 2016 by Hutton Grove
An imprint of Bravo Ltd.
Sales and Enquiries:
Kuperard Publishers & Distributors
59 Hutton Grove, London, N12 8DS
United Kingdom
Tel: +44 (0)208 446 2440
Fax: +44 (0)208 446 2441
sales@kuperard.co.uk
www.kuperard.co.uk
Published by arrangement with Albury Books
Albury Court, Albury, Oxfordshire, OX9 2LP

ISBN 978-1-910925-25-6 (hardback)
ISBN 978-1-910925-24-9 (paperback)

A CIP catalogue record for this book is available from the British Library
10 9 8 7 6 5 4 3
Printed in China

"**O**h good!" thought the naughtiest ever fairy, as a fat little envelope popped through her mailbox. "Perhaps someone has sent me a present."

But it wasn't a present. It was a letter from all of her neighbors, and this is what it said...

Dear Naughty Fairy,

STOP being so naughty! We've had enough of being turned into toads and trolls and wobbly jellies. If you don't stop your naughty tricks we will drum you out of town!

Lots of love from your friends,

Giant, Big Bad Wolf, the Butcher, the Baker, the Boiled Sweet Maker, the Three Little Pigs and the Lord Mayor

1

"**Oops,**" thought the naughtiest ever fairy. She didn't enjoy being drummed out of town, so she decided to be a well-behaved little fairy.

Starting right away!

The very noisy giant was busy
crashing around, spring-cleaning
his castle when the well-behaved
naughty fairy arrived.

"I can help you with that,"
she shouted above the noise.

GRANNY GIANT.

3

"**No!**" cried the noisy giant.
"I know your naughty tricks."
"Don't worry, I'm a well-behaved
naughty fairy." She smiled
sweetly and waved
her magic wand.

But although
the naughty
fairy tried to be
good, her magic
was determined to
be especially naughty,
and almost at once things
started to go wrong...

4

KAZAM!

Paintbrushes whizzed through the air, sloshing paint over the walls, the windows and the giant as well!

The vacuum sucked up the trash,
the rugs and just about everything else!

Soon it was so full,
it exploded in a cloud of dust.

"Sorry,"
said the good naughty fairy
and quickly flew off to help
somebody else.

6

The Big Bad Wolf was trying to huff and puff a house down.

"Oh, please let me help," volunteered the good naughty fairy, and summoned up a wind so strong it blew the wolf's clothes right off and sent the house spinning across the valley and far out to sea...

"**HELP!**"
shouted the three little pigs who were still in the house.

"**Don't worry, I'm coming,**"
cried the naughty fairy.

But on the way, she met someone else who needed her help...

8

The
boiled candy
maker lived at the
top of a steep hill and
he was mixing a huge pot
of sweet smelling candy, when
the naughty fairy passed by.

"Don't interrupt me now," puffed the candy man. "I have to finish all the candy for the Mayor's very important procession."

"Oh, let me help," cried the well-behaved naughty fairy.

And before the candy maker could shout 'No!' she had waved her magic wand.

KAZAM!

The pot began to rattle and shake, and
WOOSH! the gooey mixture erupted out
of the pot, spilling across the floor.
"**Stop it!**" cried the candy maker
as the sticky mess bubbled out of the
door and down the hill. But the
well-behaved naughty fairy
had already gone.

11

All the way down the hill, townsfolk were getting stuck in the mucky mess. The Mayor's important procession had been bought to a standstill, up to their knees in toffee.

"I should have known it was you," yelled the Mayor, shaking his fist as the naughty fairy flew by.

Soon the naughty fairy came upon the bold and roaring lion
(who was king of the jungle). He was having a royal nap.
"Ah, he's sleeping like a baby", said the helpful fairy.
"I'll just make him a little more comfortable."
She waved her magic wand and...

KAZAM!

The mighty king of the jungle awoke to find himself dressed in a baby's bonnet and diaper, rocking in a crib!

"How embarrassing," he roared.

"Just you wait!"

Big Bab

14

But by now the naughty fairy had flown out
to sea to help the three little pigs,
whose house was still bobbing
about on the waves.
"Fairy to the rescue!"
she cried, waving her
magic wand...

KAZAM!

A huge and
hungry whale
leaped out of the
sea and gobbled up the
pigs and their house
in one mouthful!

15

Up through
the clouds
it swam,
turning and
somersaulting
and emitting
polite little burps.

(A house is a substantial
meal after all, even for
an enormous whale!)

"Come back,"
called the good naughty fairy,
waving her magic wand...

16

The whale belly-flopped into the village pond.

("Oof," gasped the whale as the little pigs' house shot out of his mouth).

Pond water and pond life rained down on the town. Mrs. Munchet, the schoolteacher, was covered in slime and weeds and tadpoles...

KASPLOSH!

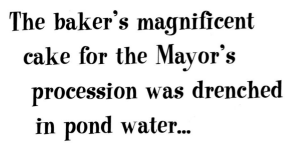

The baker's magnificent cake for the Mayor's procession was drenched in pond water...

And the last of the fiery dragon's fiery breath was snuffed out in the downpour.

"This is one of the naughty fairy's tricks," they spluttered.

18

"**Oh no!**" cried the well-behaved naughty fairy, desperately waving her magic wand as it rained frogs and salamanders.

But POP!
Her naughty magic turned one of the
frogs into her naughty new friend, who
was delighted to see the mess the
naughtiest ever fairy had made.

POP!

20

All the townspeople
marched up to the well-behaved naughty fairy.

What a state! They were covered in slime and toffee and duckweed.

(The naughty fairy couldn't help but giggle).

21

"Are you responsible for this mess?" demanded the Mayor.

"It's not my fault," complained the well-behaved naughty fairy. "I've been good, but my magic was naughty."

"Clean this mess up," ordered Mrs. Munchet.

"And no magic, or I'll turn you into a sausage!" added the naughty new friend.

Ignoring the naughty new friend, the well-behaved naughty fairy waved her magic wand to start the big clean up, but...

KAPOW!

"That's not fair," grumbled the naughtiest ever sausage, as she started the long task of mopping up.

23

"In the future I'm going
to stay naughty...

It's safer!"

24

For Jade,
Who thought I had forgotten her!

N.W.